Designed by Alan Richardson.

Published by Checkerboard Press, Inc.,
30 Vesey Street, New York, New York 10007

ISBN: 1-56288-301-1 Library of Congress Catalog Card Number: 92-71522
Printed in the U.S.A. 0 9 8 7 6 5 4 3 2 1 (F1/14)

We Can Do It!

By Laura Dwight

Checkerboard Press
New York

My name is Gina.
I am five years old.
I have spina bifida, and
I can do lots of things.

▼ I like to play
with my dollhouse.

▲ I can ride my bike.

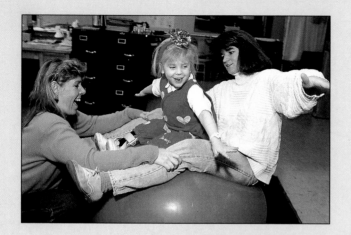

The kids want to know ▶ about my wheelchair.

▲ At school I have fun with my teachers and my friends. ▼

▲ I push my wheelchair
to the beach because
I like to play in the sand. ▶

I love the water! ▶

My name is David.
I am five years old.
I have Down syndrome, and
I can do lots of things.

▼ When my friend Richard comes
over, we play with my computer.

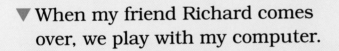Sometimes I play alone.

◀ I dress myself
and tie my own shoes.

▼ I help by setting the table.

◀ I read to my little brother and show him things.

My mom and I play games. ▶
I'm the winner!

My name is Jewel.
I am four years old.
I have cerebral palsy, and
I can do lots of things.

▲ In the greenhouse
I water the plants.

◀ I wear my new glasses
to look at books.

◄Last year I had an operation
to help me walk.

My physical therapist ►
helped me learn
to use a walker.

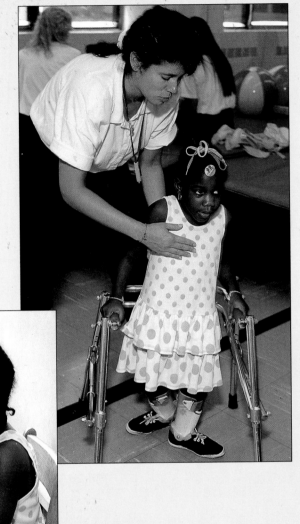

◄I have lots of fun with
my speech therapist.

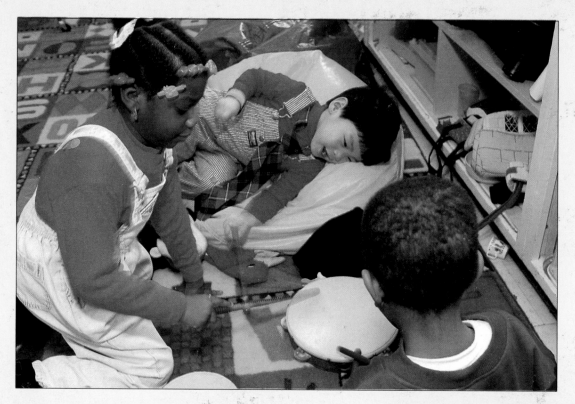

At school I make music
and build things
with my friends. ▶

Cynthia and I make our puppets wrestle and shout! ▶

When I visit Susan, my therapist, we play games that help me stand alone and make me strong.

I am the champ! ▶

My name is Sarah.
I am four years old.
I am blind, and
I can do lots of things.

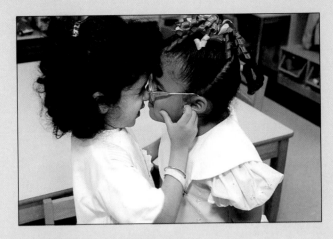

▲ This is my friend Jazmin.

▲ At school we play instruments and sing.

This is my chair.
My name is on it in
Braille. The bells help
me find it. I also have
bells on my right hand.

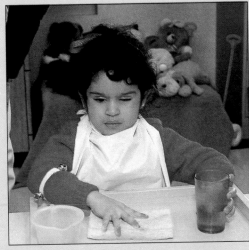

I run my fingers
along the wall so
I can tell where I
am. This is called
trailing.

I pour my own juice...   and clean up if it spills.

When my mom reads to my sister and me, I like to feel where we are in the story.

I help my dad cook—I like to make dessert!

Look at all the things we can do!

◀ Cory and Amanda

▲ Carlos and Stephen

◀ Sophie

▲ Jazmin

◀ Jennine ▲

Acknowledgements

Many children, parents, and teachers have helped with this book. I would like to give special thanks to the children in the book: Sarah Badillo, Emiliano Bourgois, Sophie Corley, Cory Cunningham, Stephen Cunningham, Cynthia Delgado, Jewel Halliday, Richard Hempel, Carlos Leon, Gina McNally, David Robards, Jazmin Ruiz, Lionel Toler, Amanda Vernuccio, and Jennine Wallace. Many thanks also to The Association for the Help of Retarded Children, Bank Street Family Center, The Children's Aid Society, The Lighthouse Child Development Center, The Lighthouse, Inc., New York City Public School 199, The New York League for Early Learning, The Rusk Institute of Rehabilitation Medicine Preschool and Infant Developmental Programs, and Ira Blank, Kirstin DeBear, Carmel and Carmel Ann Favale, Heidi Fox, Susan Scheer, Sybil Peyton, and Jodi Schiffman.

Resources

American Foundation for the Blind
15 West 16th Street
New York, NY 10011
(800) 232-5463
(212) 620-2147

National Down Syndrome Congress
1800 Dempster Street
Park Ridge, IL 60068-1146
(800) 232-6372
(312) 823-7550

National Down Syndrome Society
666 Broadway, Suite 810
New York, NY 10012
(800) 221-4602
(212) 460-9330

Resources for Children with Special Needs, Inc.
200 Park Avenue South, Suite 816
New York, NY 10003
(212) 677-4650
(*serves New York metropolitan area only*)

Spina Bifida Association of America
1700 Rockville Pile, Suite 250
Rockville, MD 20852-1654
(800) 621-3141
(301) 770-7222

United Cerebral Palsy Association
7 Penn Plaza, Suite 804
New York, NY 10001
(800) USA-IUCP
(212) 268-6655